A LETTER FROM

KRAMPUS

FOR

ka schultz

Dear _______________________

So, what is this I am hearing about you???
I heard there has been some real TROUBLE with you!!!
Now, you have probably heard, what I do with troublemakers like YOU
Do you know that those stories are utterly TRUE???
UNDERSTAND THIS, MY NEW FRIEND:
Next time when you are a-bed, when you THINK that you hear a soft tap at the window, 'twill neither be the mere branch of a tree, nor some little bird, pecking at its own shadow. . .
Oh no! 'twill be ME, coming for THEE!
for to stuff YOUR stocking first full of black coal, then to scare all that naughtiness RIGHT out of you!
So, you better watch out, and you better not cry, you better well pout, I am warning you why. . .
OLD KRAMPUS is coming to town and FOR YOU!!!

X. Krampus

A video greeting from KRAMPUS just for you!
Scan this code IF YOU DARE. . .

Now, tell me this, you impudent knave, has my
warning inspired you to at long last behave???
If you feel you're redeemed, then you may
commence with your Yule time WISH LIST!
So then, maybe, just maybe, I will magically deliver
your words from below to my old pal S. Claus up at
the North Pole. . .

Oh, but when flurries strike with such fury

By their crystalline shards the scene is so

beautifully lit

Its components snow-feathered, ice-fractiled

'tis by design, this wint'ry distraction!

from Beware of the Uhrkind

And WHAT do you promise to do BETTER
next year???
Your promises are what I, Krampus, MUST
hear!

This woodland tomb, this valley, are but a

graveyard for cast-off gods

A nave by haggard evergreens buttressed, in snowy

whorls ice christened

Spired sentinels of oak and ash, they stand, swaying

yet unmoved

Whilst I recline, keenly, agonizingly aware

Of the unfeeling universe which surrounds me. . .

from Snow's Rescue

And last but NOT least, for I am a vain BEAST, I now
command you to draw me just as you might please!
And YES make my portrait as gruesome as it could
possibly be!

Let me then fill this elegantly hollow'd and

feather'd quill

With what is left of you

So that I may craft

Khrystmass sonnets & Yuletide carols

Wint'ry odes and whispered pleadings

To honor you, my wond'rous love

Less, yes, to who you once were

More now, to this thing you have become

from Precious Inkwells

Dear Reader & next-up Krampus Host:
Do you remember that famous "Yes, Virginia, there is a Santa
Claus," as penned back in 1897 by Frances B. Church?
Well, here is its Krampian inversion . . .

Dear Editor —

I am 8 years old. Some of my little friends say there is no Krampus. Papa says, "If you see it in The Thymes, it's so." Please tell me the truth: Is there a Krampus?

Adelheid Grimm

Adelheid, your little friends are wrong. They have been afflicted by the optimism of an industrious age. They believe, even when they cannot see. They hold hope in their hearts, even if it is not fully comprehended in their guileless minds. All minds, Adelheid, be they men's or children's, are suspect. In this random and chaotic universe of ours, man is a mere rodent, an amoeba, in his intellect as compared with the stifling world about him, as measured by a stupidity capable of fomenting the whole of a lunatic & degenerate subsistence.

Yes, Adelheid, there is a Krampus. He exists as certainly as hate & selfishness & deception exist, & you know they abound to infect life, yours & mine, with its darkest nightmares & anguished tears. Alas, how simperingly sweet would be the world if there were no Krampus! It would be as superficially cheerful as a saccharin-laced Candyland. There would be no childlike misgivings then, no insults, nor dejection to make truly miserable this existence. We would have no *Schadenfreude*, but for what might infect our envious sensibilities & glare-wracked sights. Why, the very fires of hell which pollute the world would be extinguished.

Not believe in Krampus! You might as well not believe in demons. You might get your papa to bolt the cellar door, peer beneath each bed before the lights are dimmed, but even if you did not see Krampus stealing in, what would that prove? Nobody sees Krampus coming, but that is no sign that there is no Krampus. The most real things in the world are those neither villainous urchins nor murderous henchmen can see. Did you ever witness a passel of hobgoblins flailing about on the lawn? Of course not, but that's no proof that they are not there. Nobody can conceive or imagine all the terrors that are unseen & unseeable in this world.

You rip apart your bleating, pleading prey to see what makes that infernal tick- tick- ticking noise inside, but there is a veil covering the unseen world which not even the most diabolical of men, even if united in weakness, could neatly dismember. Only doubt, slurs, hate, & exploitation can push aside the tattered webbing to reveal the supernal hideousness & horror beyond. Is it all real? Ah, Adelheid, in all this world, there is nothing else as real, or abiding, or as terrorizing.

No Krampus? Great Beleth! He lives *in* death & as such will lurk forevermore in every shadowy nook, every moment of gut-twisting doubt. A thousand years from now, Adelheid, nay 10 times 10,000 years from now, he will continue to strike a most cold & wicked dread into every palpitating heart of every sleepless & fear-filled, impudent child.

Knecht X. Ruprecht

Knecht X. Ruprecht, editor
1897

This sumpt'ous wine, those twinkling lights,

Will make for a most blessèd night!

from Sibling Revelry

Indeed! The earth is phenomenally beautiful, and for all the seasons I have seen pass in my day, I have never grown tired of observing every changing of that cyclical guard, least of all the dying off of life when winter sets in, that miraculous stasis before the next turnover to another birth, a reanimated emergence.

The *Polarlichter* – such a symphony of pleasing color! And how they waltz across the heavens. . . I watch for them, especially when the autumn sets in, when the lights are re-ignited as if by fire. It is very nearly enough to justify one's hanging on for yet another year. And I say this as one who has trod over ages and their countless miles, heavily burdened for the most part, where their beauty was, at times, what kept me going. . .

From, "Stille Nacht" KHRYSTMASS

A LETTER FROM

KRAMPUS

K.A. Schultz

Dakeha Taunus LLC, publisher
Copyright 2024 by K.A. Schultz
ALL RIGHTS RESERVED

A LETTER FROM KRAMPUS is a work of fiction. Any resemblances
to actual people, living or dead, places or events,
are coincidental. Poetry outtakes are from KHRYSTMASS

No AI was used in the creation or execution of this literary work.

Inquiries may be addressed to butterflybroth@gmail.com

https://linktr.ee/K.A.SchultZ

ISBN 979-8-9894856-8-0 Ingram paperback

*Poetry and text excerpts are from
the following books,
also by K.A. Schultz*

KHRYSTMASS – Holiday Horror Collection 2024

GÖTHIQUE – Ravenscraft Anthology of Horror III 2023

NEITHERIUM – Prose & Poetry from the Neither 2022

JACOB – A Denouement in One Act 2019

RUGS ON PUDDLES COATS OVER OCEANS –
Poems & Lyric Poetry 2013

All books are available at Amazon and via Ingram
First edition illustrated hardback of JACOB is available at eBay

Dakeha Taunus LLC, publisher

www.butterflybroth.com
www.jacobmarleystory.com
www.shewhowas.com

@kaschultz_writer
@butterflybroth
@lilahravenscraft

 linktr.ee/K.A.Schultz